Frank's Great
Museum Adventure

by ROD CLEMENT

HarperCollins*Publishers*

Frank's Great
Museum Adventure

Every morning is an adventure for me, a journey of discovery. Finding clean clothes isn't enough. I want more.

So today I'm going to travel in time and explore the past. I don't mean looking at faded photos of your grandparents or searching for the old sandwich under the bed. I mean the really old stuff.

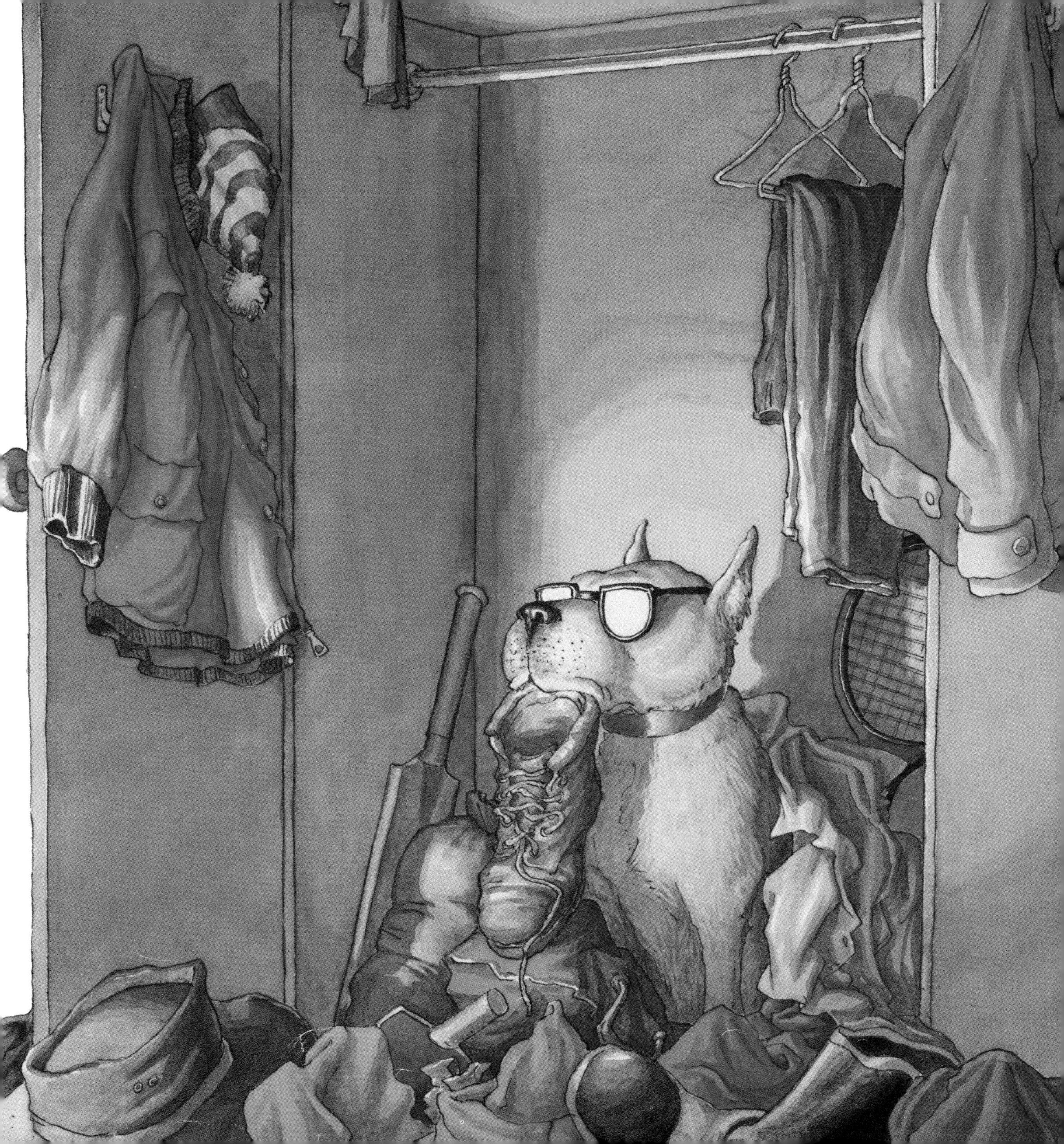

Traveling in time is not as hard as you think.
All you need is a backpack, good walking shoes,
and two tickets to the museum.

Yes, folks, the museum.
There's more old stuff in that place than you will ever find
in your attic or between the cushions of your couch!

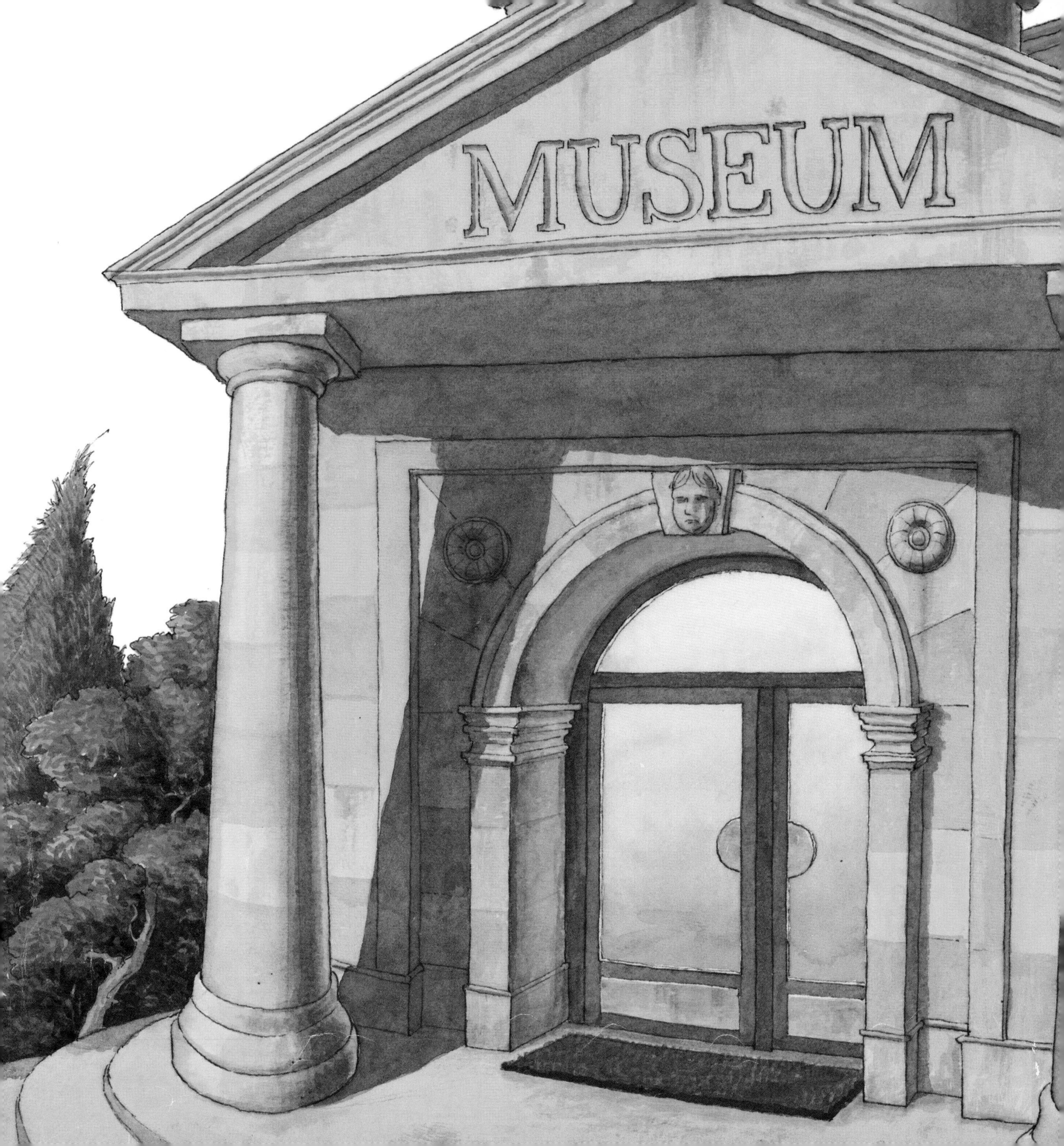
MUSEUM

Walking through the front door is like walking into history. The first thing you see is a skeleton of a man standing next to a skeleton of a dinosaur. They look like they're going for a stroll.

The dinosaur must be well trained.

I wonder if he goes to obedience classes like Frank?

In the first display is a sculpture of the Ice Age. It looks just like the inside of our freezer.

Perhaps the same scientists who found the frozen woolly mammoth could look for the ham and pineapple pizza we lost a few years ago.

ICE

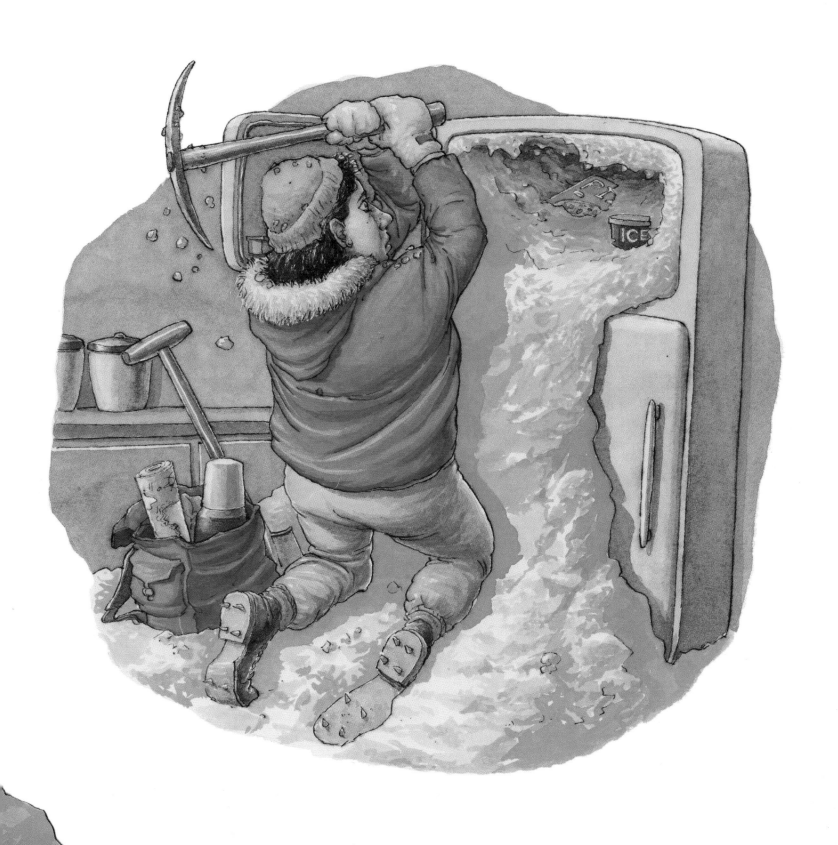

Did you know that primitive man was covered in hair and made tools out of stone?

Just imagine if all your tools were made of stone— the tool kits must have weighed a ton!

They obviously couldn't make scissors out of stone.
The hairstyles were terrible.

Egyptians were different. They cared about their appearance. In fact, they cared so much about their looks, they wanted to keep them forever, even after they died! That's why all the mummies were wrapped up in bandages—to protect their skin.

I wonder where all the daddies were?

If they were anything like my dad, they were probably all back in the pyramids watching sports on TV.

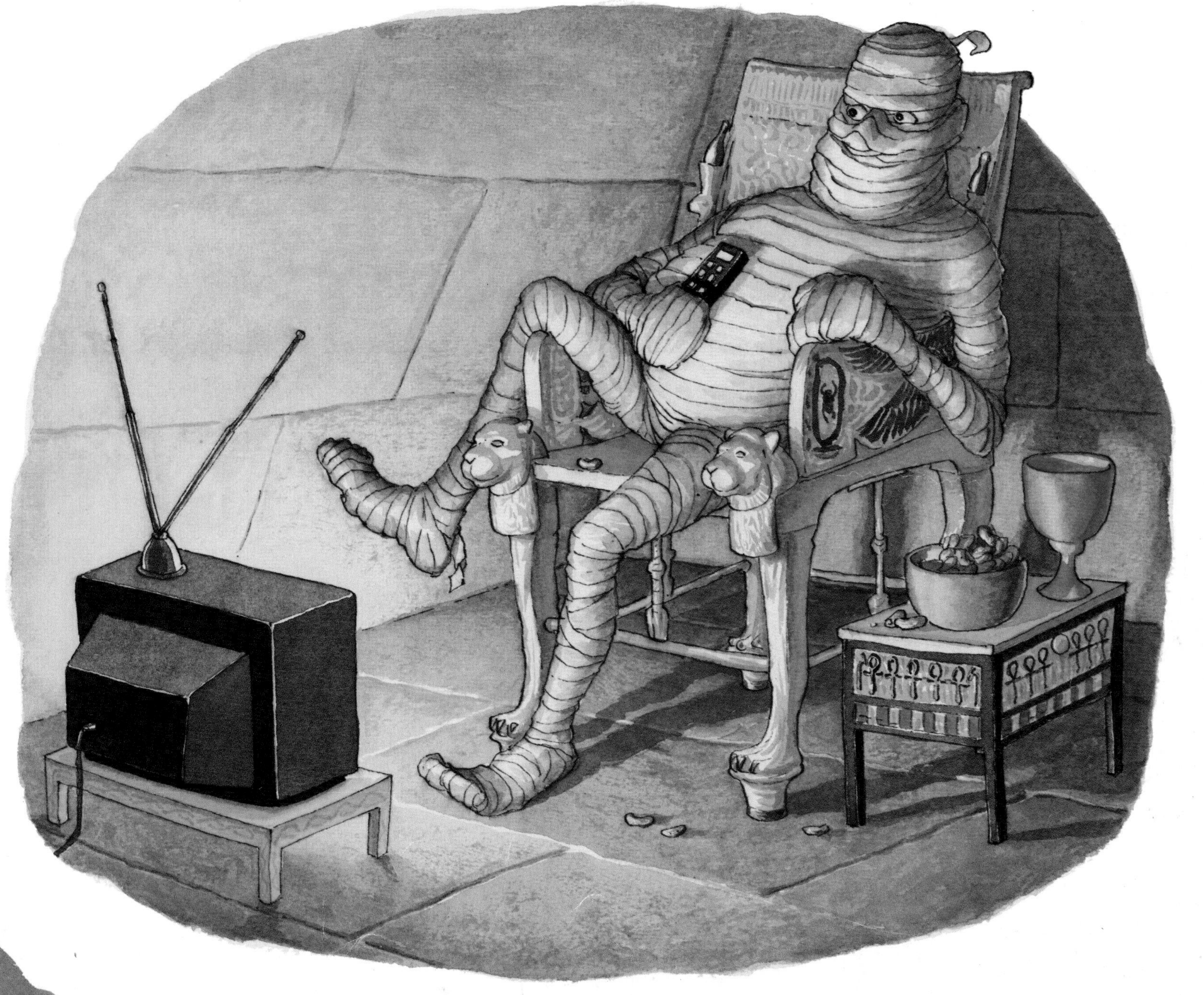

The Romans loved sports so much that they built one of the earliest stadiums, the amphitheater. Thousands of spectators would sit in the stands and cheer as their favorite gladiators fought to the death.

It's a pity we don't have that extra protection now. It would be so much easier to avoid door-to-door salesmen.

Finding things was a full-time job for Christopher Columbus. He sailed halfway around the world to find America and he didn't even have the address.

I wish he were alive today—he could sail halfway around the world again and find Mom's car keys.

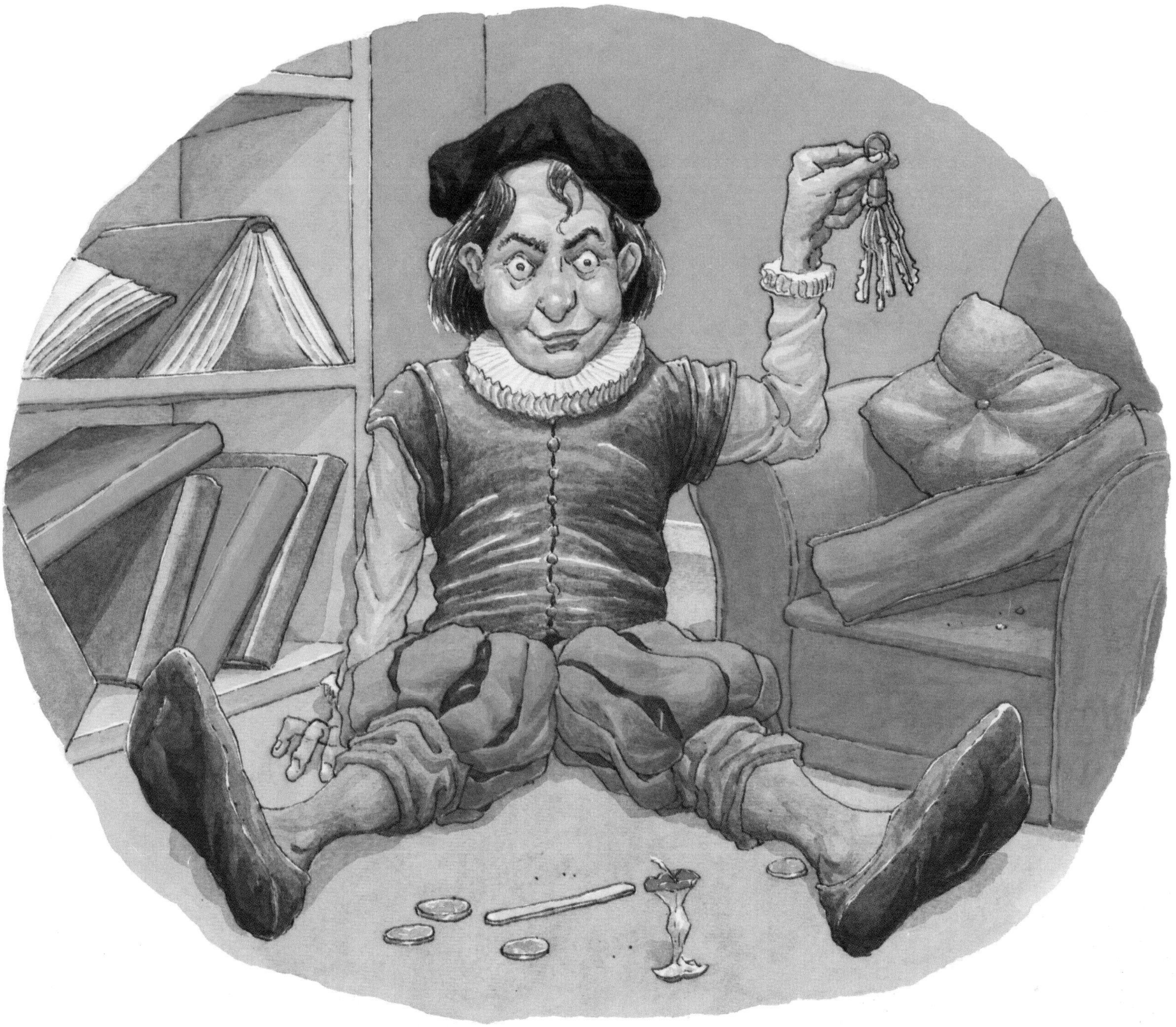

You don't have to be on the move to discover things.
Isaac Newton was hit on the head by an apple while
sitting under a tree, and discovered gravity.

Lucky he wasn't sitting under a coconut tree—
he could have been seriously hurt.

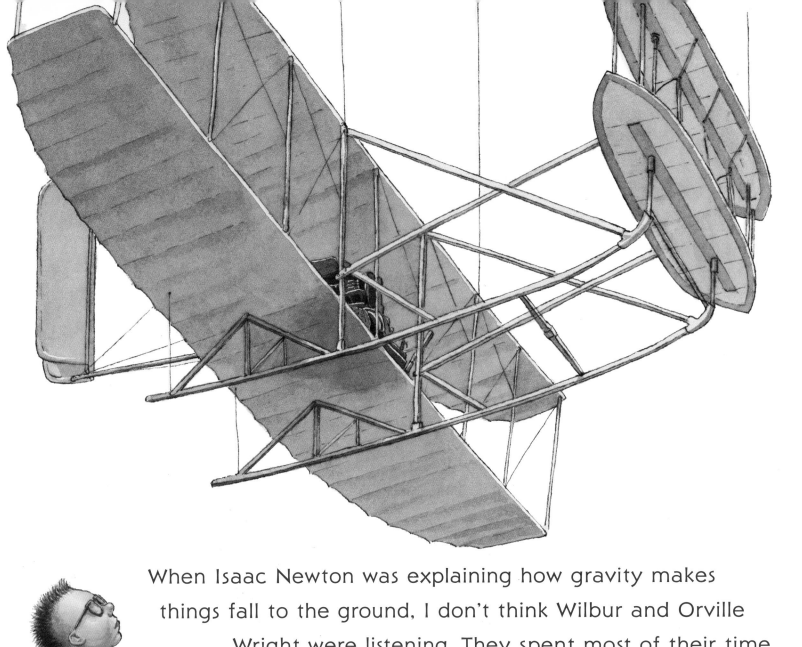

When Isaac Newton was explaining how gravity makes things fall to the ground, I don't think Wilbur and Orville Wright were listening. They spent most of their time trying to get off the ground and stay off.

After a lot of practice, they managed to stay off the ground for 59 seconds, which is about the same as my record-breaking paper-plane flight.

If they had used my design, all they would have needed was a huge piece of paper and an enormous hand.

Once people learned to fly, there was no stopping them.
Getting off the ground wasn't enough—they wanted to get to the moon.
They went all that way to leave a flag and some footprints.

That's a long way to go just to make some footprints.
It would have been a lot easier just to make them in
the cement that runs down our street.

So here we are back where we started, after exploring 12,000 years of history. It wasn't too hard—no scratches, bruises, or serious illness, and still half a bar of chocolate left.

It's great to know how things have changed and how people have changed them. Anyone can change things if they try hard enough—even Frank.

So how can I make history?

"That's easy," said my dad. "You could be the first kid in the world to keep his room tidy."

I agree. That's why I've decided to design and build
the world's first automatic room tidier.
Tidy the room—then the world!

First published in Australia by Angus & Robertson,
an imprint of HarperCollins Publishers.

Frank's Great Museum Adventure
Copyright © 1998 by Rod Clement
http://www.harperchildrens.com

Library of Congress Cataloging-in-Publication Data
Clement, Rod.
    Frank's great museum adventure / Rod Clement.
        p.   cm.
    Summary: Frank the dog and his owner travel through history when they
visit the museum.
    ISBN 0-06-027673-8. — ISBN 0-06-027674-6 (lib. bdg.)
    [1. Museums—Fiction.   2. Dogs—Fiction.]   I. Title.
PZ7.C59114Fr   1999   98-441710
[E]—dc21   CIP
                                                                                  AC

Typography by Elynn Cohen
1   2   3   4   5   6   7   8   9   10
❖
First American edition, 1999